PACO AND THE WITCH

A Puerto Rican Folktale

RETOLD BY Felix Pitre

ILLUSTRATED BY Christy Hale

Lodestar Books

DUTTON   NEW YORK

for my loving wife, Marion,
and our two sons, Felix III and Brandon,
who never seem to tire of Dad's stories
F.P.

for my mother, Eunice Sherman Hale
C.H.

Also by FELIX PITRE

JUAN BOBO AND THE PIG
illustrated by CHRISTY HALE

Text copyright © 1995 by Felix Pitre
Illustrations copyright © 1995 by Christy Hale

Library of Congress Cataloging-in-Publication Data
Pitre, Felix.
    Paco and the witch: a Puerto Rican folktale/retold by Felix Pitre;
illustrated by Christy Hale.—1st ed.
        p.   cm.
    Summary: A young boy is trapped by a crafty witch who will not
free him unless he can guess her name.
    ISBN 0-525-67501-9
    [1.Folklore—Puerto Rico.]   I. Hale, Christy, ill.   II. Title.
PZ8.1.P683Pac   1995
398.2—dc20
[E]
                                                    94-20532
                                                        CIP
                                                         AC

Published in the United States by Lodestar Books,
an affiliate of Dutton Children's Books,
a division of Penguin Books USA Inc.,
375 Hudson Street, New York, New York 10014

Published simultaneously in Canada
by McClelland & Stewart, Toronto

Editor: Rosemary Brosnan   Designer: Christy Hale
Printed in Hong Kong
First Edition 10 9 8 7 6 5 4 3 2 1

AUTHOR'S NOTE

When I first started telling stories more than twenty years ago, this one quickly became a favorite with audiences. Pura Belpré, a wonderful Puerto Rican storyteller and writer, included it in her anthology *The Tiger and the Rabbit* under the title "Casi Lampu'a Lentemué." Recently I had the opportunity to view her papers at the Center for Puerto Rican Studies at New York City's Hunter College. That experience left me with a sense of kinship to and appreciation for a countryman I had never met but in whose debt I remain.

This story is much more than a Puerto Rican version of "Rumpelstiltskin," for it also represents the rich culture of the island where I was born. I have developed Paco's relationships to his family and his culture and added the *cotorra* (parrot) and the *coquí* (Puerto Rican frog). And, of course, there is the foreboding wood, symbolic of the beauty and mystery of this exotic land where *la bruja*, the sorceress, dwells, embodying the myths and ceremonies of the native Taínos and Caribes with their rituals of enchantment and cannibalism.

When I returned to Puerto Rico as an adult after leaving at age two and walked along a central mountain path in Yauco, I was overcome with a deep sense of belonging—to the people, the land, and the creatures, past and present, that were calling me their own. I invite the reader to journey on this path with me and share that experience.

GLOSSARY

abuela (ah-DWAY-lah) — grandmother

agua (AH-gwah) — water

aguinaldos (ah-ghee-NAHL-dohs) — Puerto Rican folksongs

ahora (ah-OH-rah) — now

bebé (beh-BAY) — baby

bodega (boh-DAY-gah) — grocery store

borras (BOR-rahs) — coffee grounds

bruja (BREW-hah) — witch

café (ka-FAY) — coffee

caliente (kah-li-EN-tay) — hot

cangrejo (kahn-GREH-hoh) — crab

carne (KAR-nay) — meat

Casi Lampu'a Lentemué (KAH-see Lahm-POO-ah Len-teh-moo-AY)

¿cómo estás? (KOH-moh ess-TAHS) — how are you?

coquí (koh-KEE) — Puerto Rican frog

cotorra (koh-TOHR-rah) — parrot

de lejos (deh LEH-hohs) — from afar

fiesta (fee-ES-tah) — party

flamboyán (flahm-boh-YAHN) — royal poinciana tree

gandules (gahn-DOO-less) — pigeon peas

güiro (GWEE-roh) — gourd instrument

guitarra (ghee-TAHR-rah) — guitar

hola (OH-lah) — hello

jíbaros (HEE-bah-rohs) — Puerto Rican country people

leña (LEN-yah) — firewood

mamá (mah-MAH) — mother

molí (moh-LEE) — I crushed into fine particles

muchas gracias (MOO-chas GRAH-see-ahs) — thank you very much

muy bien (mwee bee-YEN) — very well

muy fácil (mwee FAH-seel) — very easy

Niño ¿por qué lloras? (NEEN-yoh, por KAY yoh-rahs) — Little boy, why are you crying?

nombre (NOME-bray) — name

pasteles (pahs-TEH-less) — green banana-and-meat pies

por favor (pore fah-VORE) — please

qué casa más bonita (kay KAH-sah mahs boh-NEE-tah) — what a beautiful house

qué nombre más dulce (kay NOHM-breh mahs DOOL-seh) — what a sweet name

refresco (reh-FRES-koh) — cool drink

río (REE-oh) — river

señor (sen-YORE) — mister

sol (sole) — sun

tío (TEE-oh) — uncle

turrón (too-RRONE) — candy made of wafers and nougat

usted (oos-TED) — you (formal)

viejita (vee-eh-HEE-tah) — an old woman

yo sé (yoh say) — I know

Many years ago a little boy named Paco
lived on the island of Puerto Rico. He shared a small
house high up in the hills with his mother, father, sisters,
and brothers. Separating their house from the village was a wood
filled with many wild and beautiful animals. The children loved to
play by the edge of the woods, but they never went far from the
road that led to the village because of the story their *abuela*, their
grandmother, had told them. It was about *una bruja*, a witch, who
lived deep within the forest. She was always ready to snatch up
some careless child, who would never be seen again. Many
nights Paco sat looking out of his bedroom window at the
dark woods below, wondering about his *abuela*'s story.

But on this day there was no time to think about *brujas*. Tonight there was to be *una fiesta*, with many friends and relatives. Tío Julio, Paco's uncle, always brought *su guitarra*, his guitar. Father would then reach for his favorite instrument, *el güiro*, a beautifully decorated gourd that hung on the living room wall. Soon *aguinaldos*, happy folksongs of the country people, *los jíbaros*, would fill the evening air.

Everyone was busy preparing for *la fiesta*. Paco was helping his mother make *pasteles*. He was grinding green bananas while she made the meat sauce filling. Suddenly she dropped her spoon and gasped, "*¡Ay, no!* I forgot *el turrón* that Don Santiago ordered for me!" Paco loved this candy of wafers and nougat that Señor Santiago, who owned *la bodega*, the grocery store in town, shipped in from Spain. He got to taste it only on special occasions. "I will get *el turrón*, Mamá," Paco said. And after being told to go straight to town and not stop on the way, Paco set off for Don Santiago's bodega.

In Puerto Rico *el sol*, the sun, shines very brightly, and it feels *muy caliente*, very hot. After walking down the road awhile, Paco felt hot and tired. *Ay*, maybe I'll sit down on this rock and rest a little, he thought.

Just at that moment, someone who had been standing quietly behind a tree strolled over, singing "*Le lo lai, le lo lai. Hola, Paco. ¿Cómo estás?* How are you?"

Paco was so surprised to hear a voice that he jumped off the rock with a scream. But when he turned to look he saw that it was . . .

just *una viejita*, a little old woman. "*Hola, ¿cómo está usted?* Hello, how are you?" he asked politely.

"Oh, Paco," she said, sounding very concerned, "you look so *caliente*. Why don't you come into my house for *un refresco*, a cool drink?"

Paco's throat felt so dry, and he thought, I'd love to have *un refresco*, but my parents said I shouldn't stop anywhere. Should I have a drink? Maybe just a little drink?

"It won't take long, Paco," cooed the old woman sweetly.

I'll just have a little drink, thought Paco. He followed the old woman into the woods, along a winding road that led to a small house. Once inside, Paco could not believe his eyes. "*¡Qué casa más bonita!* What a pretty house!"

The old woman poured Paco a cool drink, saying some words to herself that he could not understand. "*Muchas gracias*, thank you," replied Paco as he held the cup and licked his dry lips. He still wasn't sure as he asked himself, "Should I drink it?" But he was thirsty, and the woman did seem so nice, and so, he DRANK IT!

Paco was thinking that *el refresco*
tasted great and his throat felt much
better, when he began to feel something
hot in his stomach that grew stronger and
stronger until he doubled over in pain.

　　　Suddenly the old woman threw off her shawl,
and he saw her ugly face as she laughed and screamed
at him, "Now I've got you, Paco. You will be mine
forever. You will never leave these woods unless
you can guess *mi nombre*, my name!"

"¡La bruja!" cried Paco. "It's the witch! Abuela was right!" He was under her spell. His heart sank, for he felt that he would never see his home again. Paco began to weep.

"Now you must work!" cried the witch. Go and bring me some *leña*, firewood. Go!" Paco went sadly into the woods. As he gathered *la leña*, he tried to think of a fitting name for the witch.

Then the witch called him into the house, and since he was under her spell, he had to obey.

"Here is *su leña*," he said meekly.

"All right!" cackled the witch. "What is *mi nombre*, my name?"

Paco thought and thought. "Well, could it be Estor?"

"Oh, what a lovely name," said the witch sweetly. "But the answer is nooooo!" And she screamed with delight as she danced around the room.

Soon the witch looked at Paco with an ugly, toothless grin and said, "Now you must go out into the fields behind my house and bring me *gandules*, pigeon peas, for my stew. Go!" With heavy shoulders, Paco found his way to the fields and gathered *gandules* for the witch.

He knew he had to come up with her name, but what could it be?

"Paco! Paco!" the witch screeched. "Come in here now! *¡Ahora!*"

"Here," Paco said, trying to hold back his tears. "Here are *sus gandules.*"

"*Muy bien*, very well, this is your second chance. What is *mi nombre?*" asked the witch with great anticipation.

"I'll tell you what it is," shot back Paco. "It's . . . it's Katerina!"

This time the witch brought her face so close to Paco's that he could feel her hot breath and see the glow in her eyes. Quietly, she whispered, "Katerina? *¡Qué nombre más dulce!* What a sweet name! But I'm afraid the answer is . . . noooooooo!" And she screamed and danced as never before until the house began to shake.

When she had tired of dancing, she looked at Paco and hissed, "Now, Paco, this is your last chance. Go to *el río*, the river, and bring me some *agua*, water, so that I may prepare my stew of *gandules con carne*."

"*¿Con carne?*" asked Paco. Where are you going to get meat for your stew?"

"Oh, that's a surprise, Paco," answered the witch slyly. "You'll find out after you've had your last chance. Now get my water. Go!"

Paco took a pail and headed for the river. He was feeling so sad that he could barely drag himself to the riverbank. When he got there he fell to his knees and began to cry.

As he wept, Paco thought about his home and family.
He didn't mind missing *la fiesta* or even *el turrón*. He
just wanted to be home again helping Mamá in the kitchen
or listening to Papá play *su güiro*. He longed to see his
brothers and sisters, even if they did tease him. Paco
realized how important these things were to him.

Just then, strolling along the riverbank, came *un cangrejo*, a crab, who was waving his claws in the air and singing joyfully to himself, *"Dai de dai dai. Dai de dai dai."*

When he saw Paco, the crab froze and asked him, *"Niño, ¿por qué lloras?* Little boy, why are you crying?"

"Oh, Señor Cangrejo," Paco sobbed, "I'm crying because this *bruja* has trapped me and won't let me go unless I guess her name."

"Oh, is that all?" said the crab, scratching his head with a claw. "I know the witch's name. But you mustn't let her know who told you."

"Don't worry, I won't tell," cried Paco. *"Por favor,* what is *su nombre?"*

"Her name is . . . Casi Lampu'a . . . Lentemué!" answered the crab.

"Casi Lampu'a Lente . . . whaa?" Paco replied.

"Casi Lampu'a Lentemué . . . *¡Olé!"* sang the crab.

"Casi Lampu'a Lentemué, *¡Olé!"* repeated Paco with a smile.

Paco and the crab danced as they sang the witch's name again and again.

"Muchas gracias, Señor Cangrejo," said Paco, joyfully shaking the crab's claw.

When he returned to the witch's house, Paco defiantly faced
her and said, "Here is your *agua*."

"Now, Paco," she replied, "this is your last chance. Before I
make my stew, give me your answer. What is *mi nombre?*"

"I know your name," Paco shouted at the witch. "Your name
is Casi Lampu'a . . . uh, uh . . . " Paco tried hard to think of
the last part, and then it came to him: "Lentemué! *¡Olé!*"

The witch, who had started to dance and was about to scream,
looked at Paco in disbelief. Only her lips moved as she repeated
the name: "Casi Lampu'a Lentemué, oh, noooooooo!"

With that the spell was broken.
The doors of the house flew open,
and Paco ran all the way home.
"I'm free! I'm free!" he shouted,
waving his arms in the air.

But the witch was angry.
She grabbed a big stick and
went to find out who had told Paco
her name. "Whooooooooo? Whooooooooo?"
she screamed as she ran through the woods.

First she came to *la cotorra*, the parrot, who was perched
in a *flamboyán* tree, preening her beautiful coat of red, yellow,
and green feathers. The witch looked up at the parrot and said:

> *¡Cotorra! ¡Cotorra!*
>
> Coffee grounds are *borras!*
>
> Who told Paco my name?

The parrot stopped preening, looked at the witch, and
squawked:

> I know, *yo sé,*
>
> Coffee is *café,*
>
> But don't blame me
>
> If Paco's free!

The witch gave a shrug of disgust and headed toward
the river. Suddenly, she came across *el coquí*, the tiny frog
who lives only in Puerto Rico. *El coquí* was singing
sweetly, crouched upon a leaf. This time she said:

> ¡Coquí! ¡Coquí!
>
> To grind we say *molí!*
>
> Who told Paco my name?

El coquí stopped singing long enough to say:

> I know, *yo sé*,
>
> A baby is *bebé*,
>
> But singing your name
>
> Is not my game!

The anger growing inside her burst forth in a frightful
scream, and the witch continued on until she came to
el río, where she met the crab, to whom she growled:

¡Cangrejo! ¡Cangrejo!

Afar we say, *ide lejos!*

Who told Paco my name?

And the crab, who loved to play rhyming games,

didn't realize what he was saying as he replied:

Casi! Casi!
It's easy, *ies muy fácil!*
I'm brave and I'm bold
And your name I told!

As soon as the words were out of his mouth the crab knew
he had made a terrible mistake. The witch gave a shriek
and raised her stick to beat him. Luckily he managed to run
underneath a rock before she could land a blow.

That night, as
Paco sat by his
bedroom window
looking down at the woods,
he thought about his adventure.
His brothers and sisters refused to believe
his story, but Paco knew it was true. And it was.
For to this day, in Puerto Rico, if you go by the
river and see a crab, he won't stop to talk anymore.
Instead, he runs underneath a rock because he thinks
the witch sent you to beat him for telling Paco that
her name was Casi Lampu'a Lentemué! *¡Olé!*